WAR ON BEAR CREEK

BY

ROBERT E. HOWARD

British Library Cataloguing-in-Publication Data
A catalogue record for this book is available from the
British Library

Robert E. Howard

Robert Ervin Howard was born in Peaster, Texas in 1906. During his youth, his family moved between a variety of Texan boomtowns, and Howard – a bookish and somewhat introverted child – was steeped in the violent myths and legends of the Old South. Although he loved reading and learning, Howard developed a distinctly Texan, hardboiled outlook on the world. He became a passionate fan of boxing, taking it up at an amateur level, and from the age of nine began to write adventure tales of semi-historical bloodshed. In 1919, when Howard was thirteen, his family moved to the Central Texas hamlet of Cross Plains, where he would stay for the rest of his life.

At fifteen Howard began to read the pulp magazines of the day, and to write more seriously. The December 1922 issue of his high school newspaper featured two of his stories, 'Golden Hope Christmas' and 'West is West'. In 1924 he sold his first piece – a short caveman tale titled 'Spear and Fang' – for $16 to the not-yet-famous *Weird Tales* magazine. He published with the magazine regularly over the next few years. 1929 was a breakout year for Howard, in that the 23-year-old writer began to sell to other magazines, such as *Ghost Stories* and *Argosy*, both of whom had previously sent him hundreds of rejection slips. In 1930, he began a correspondence with weird fiction master H. P. Lovecraft which ran up to his death six years later, and is regarded as one of the great correspondence cycles in all of fantasy literature.

It was partly due to Lovecraft's encouragement that Howard created his most famous character, Conan the Cimmerian. Conan – a barbarian-turned-King during the Hyborian Age, a mythical period of some 12,000 years ago – featured in seventeen *Weird Tales* stories between 1933 and 1936, and is now regarded as having spawned the 'sword and sorcery' genre, making Howard's influence on fantasy literature comparable to that of J. R. R. Tolkien's. The Conan stories have since been adapted many times, most famously in the series of films starring Arnold Schwarzenegger.

Howard was enjoying an all-time high in sales by the beginning of 1936, but he was also deeply upset by the ill health of his mother, who had fallen into a coma. On the morning of June 11, 1936, he asked an attending nurse whether she would ever recover, and the nurse replied negatively. Howard walked to his car, parked outside the family home in Cross Plains, and shot himself. He died eight hours later, aged just thirty.

Pap dug the nineteenth buckshot out of my shoulder and said, "Pigs is more disturbin' to the peace of a community than scandal, divorce, and corn licker put together. And," says pap, pausing to strop his bowie on my scalp where the hair was all burnt off, "when the pig is a razorback hawg, and is mixed up with a lady schoolteacher, a English tenderfoot, and a passle of bloodthirsty relatives, the result is appallin' for a peaceable man to behold. Hold still till John gits yore ear sewed back on."

Pap was right. I warn't to blame for what happened. Breaking Joel Gordon's laig was a mistake, and Erath Elkins is a liar when he says I caved in them five ribs of his'n plumb on purpose. If Uncle Jeppard Grimes had been tending to his own business he wouldn't have got the seat of his britches filled with bird-shot, and I don't figger it was my fault that cousin Bill Kirby's cabin got burned down. And I don't take no blame for Jim Gordon's ear which Jack Grimes shot off, neither. I figger everybody was more to blame than I was, and I stand ready to wipe up the earth with anybody which disagrees with me.

But it was that derned razorback hawg of Uncle Jeppard Grimes' which started the whole mess.

It begun when that there tenderfoot come riding up the trail with Tunk Willoughby, from War Paint. Tunk ain't got no more sense than the law allows, but he shore showed good jedgement that time, because having delivered his charge to his destination, he didn't tarry. He merely handed me a note, and p'inted dumbly at the tenderfoot, whilst holding his hat reverently in his hand meanwhile.

"What you mean by that there gesture?" I ast him rather irritably, and he said: "I doffs my sombrero in respect to the departed. Bringin' a specimen like that onto Bear Creek is just like heavin' a jackrabbit to a pack of starvin' loboes."

He hove a sigh and shook his head, and put his hat back on. "Rassle a cat in pieces," he says, gathering up the reins.

"What the hell are you talkin' about?" I demanded.

"That's Latin," he said. "It means rest in peace."

And with that he dusted it down the trail and left me alone with the tenderfoot which all the time was setting his cayuse and looking at me like I was a curiosity or something.

I called my sister Ouachita to come read that there note for me, which she did and it run as follows:

Dere Breckinridge:

This will interjuice Mr. J. Pembroke Pemberton a English sportsman which I met in Frisco recent. He was disapinted because he hadn't found no adventures in America and was fixin to go to Aferker to shoot liuns and elerfants but I perswaded him to come with me because I knowed he would find more hell on Bear Creek in a week than he would find in a yere in Aferker or any other place. But the very day we hit War Paint I run into a old ackwaintance from Texas I will not speak no harm of the ded but I wish the son of a buzzard had shot me somewheres besides in my left laig which already had three slugs in it which I never could get cut out. Anyway I am lade up and not able to come on to Bear Creek with J. Pembroke Pemberton. I am dependin on you to show him some good bear huntin and other excitement and pertect him from yore relatives I know what a awful responsibility I am puttin on you but I am askin' this as yore frend.

William Harrison Glanton. Esqy.

I looked J. Pembroke over. He was a medium sized young feller and looked kinda soft in spots. He had yaller hair and very pink cheeks like a gal; and he had on whip-cord britches and tan riding boots which was the first I ever seen. And he had on a funny kinda coat with pockets and a belt which he called a shooting jacket, and a big hat like a mushroom made outa cork with a red ribbon around it. And he had a pack-horse loaded with all kinds of plunder, and four or five different kinds of shotguns and rifles.

"So yo're J. Pembroke," I says, and he says, "Oh, rahther! And you, no doubt, are the person Mr. Glanton described to me, Breckinridge Elkins?"

"Yeah," I said. "Light and come in. We got b'ar meat and honey for supper."

"I say," he said, climbing down. "Pardon me for being a bit personal, old chap, but may I ask if your-ah-magnitude of bodily stature is not a bit unique?"

"I dunno," I says, not having the slightest idee what he was talking about. "I always votes a straight Democratic ticket, myself."

He started to say something else, but just then pap and my brothers John and Bill and Jim and Buckner and Garfield come to the door to see what the noise was about, and he turned pale and said faintly: "I beg your pardon; giants seem to be the rule in these parts."

"Pap says men ain't what they was when he was in his prime," I said, "but we manage to git by."

Well, J. Pembroke laid into them b'ar steaks with a hearty will, and when I told him we'd go after b'ar next day, he ast me how many days travel it'd take till we got to the b'ar country.

"Heck!" I said. "You don't have to travel to git b'ar in these parts. If you forgit to bolt yore door at night yo're liable to find a grizzly sharin' yore bunk before mornin'. This here'n we're eatin' was ketched by my sister Ellen there whilst tryin' to rob the pig-pen out behind the cabin last night."

"My word!" he says, looking at her peculiarly. "And may I ask, Miss Elkins, what caliber of firearm you used?"

"I knocked him in the head with a wagon tongue," she said, and he shook his head to hisself and muttered: "Extraordinary!"

J. PEMBROKE SLEPT IN my bunk and I took the floor that night; and we was up at daylight and ready to start after the b'ar. Whilst J. Pembroke was fussing over his guns, pap come out and pulled his whiskers and shook his head and said: "That there is a perlite young man, but I'm afeared he ain't as hale as he oughta be. I just give him a pull at my jug, and he didn't gulp but one good snort and like to choked to death."

"Well," I said, buckling the cinches on Cap'n Kidd, "I've done learnt not to jedge outsiders by the way they takes their licker on Bear Creek. It takes a Bear Creek man to swig Bear Creek corn juice."

"I hopes for the best," sighed pap. "But it's a dismal sight to see a young man which cain't stand up to his licker. Whar you takin' him?"

"Over toward Apache Mountain," I said. "Erath seen a exter big grizzly over there day before yesterday."

"Hmmmm!" says pap. "By pecooliar coincidence the schoolhouse is over on the side of Apache Mountain, ain't it, Breckinridge?"

"Maybe it is and maybe it ain't," I replied with dignerty, and rode off with J. Pembroke ignoring pap's sourcastic comment which he hollered after me: "Maybe they is a connection between book-larnin' and b'ar-huntin', but who am I to say?"

J. Pembroke was a purty good rider, but he used a funny looking saddle without no horn nor cantle, and he had the derndest gun I ever seen. It was a double-barrel rifle, and he said it was a elerfant-gun. It was big enough to knock a hill down. He was surprised I didn't tote no rifle and ast me what would I do if we met a b'ar. I told him I was depending on him to shoot it, but I said if it was necessary for me to go into action, my six-shooter was plenty.

"My word!" says he. "You mean to say you can bring down a grizzly with a shot from a pistol?"

"Not always," I said. "Sometimes I have to bust him over the head with the butt to finish him."

He didn't say nothing for a long time after that.

Well, we rode over on the lower slopes of Apache Mountain, and tied the horses in a holler and went through the bresh on foot. That was a good place for b'ars, because they come there very frequently looking for Uncle Jeppard Grimes' pigs which runs loose all over the lower slopes of the mountain.

But just like it always is when yo're looking for something, we didn't see a cussed b'ar.

The middle of the evening found us around on the south side of the mountain where they is a settlement of Kirbys and Grimeses and Gordons. Half a dozen families has their cabins within a mile of each other, and I dunno what in hell they want to crowd up together that way for, it would plumb smother me, but pap says they was always peculiar that way.

We warn't in sight of the settlement, but the schoolhouse warn't far off, and I said to J. Pembroke: "You wait here a while and maybe a b'ar will come by. Miss Margaret Ashley is teachin' me how to read and write, and it's time for my lesson."

I left J. Pembroke setting on a log hugging his elerfant-gun, and I strode through the bresh and come out at the upper end of the run which the settlement was at the other'n, and school had just turned out and the chillern was going home, and Miss Ashley was waiting for me in the log schoolhouse.

That was the first school that was ever taught on Bear Creek, and she was the first teacher. Some of the folks was awful sot agen it at first, and said no good would come of book larning, but after I licked six or seven of them they allowed it might be a good thing after all, and agreed to let her take a whack at it.

Miss Margaret was a awful purty gal and come from somewhere away back East. She was setting at her hand-made desk as I come in, ducking my head so as not to bump it agen the top of the door and perlitely taking off my coonskin cap. She looked kinda tired and discouraged, and

I said: "Has the young'uns been raisin' any hell today, Miss Margaret?"

"Oh, no," she said. "They're very polite-in fact I've noticed that Bear Creek people are always polite except when they're killing each other. I've finally gotten used to the boys wearing their bowie knives and pistols to school. But somehow it seems so futile. This is all so terribly different from everything to which I've always been accustomed. I get discouraged and feel like giving up."

"You'll git used to it," I consoled her. "It'll be a lot different once yo're married to some honest reliable young man."

She give me a startled look and said: "Married to someone here on Bear Creek?"

"Shore," I said, involuntarily expanding my chest under my buckskin shirt. "Everybody is just wonderin' when you'll set the date. But le's git at the lesson. I done learnt the words you writ out for me yesterday."

But she warn't listening, and she said: "Do you have any idea of why Mr. Joel Grimes and Mr. Esau Gordon quit calling on me? Until a few days ago one or the other was at Mr. Kirby's cabin where I board almost every night."

"Now don't you worry none about them," I soothed her. "Joel'll be about on crutches before the week's out, and Esau can already walk without bein' helped. I always handles my relatives as easy as possible."

10

"You fought with them?" she exclaimed.

"I just convinced 'em you didn't want to be bothered with 'em," I reassured her. "I'm easy-goin', but I don't like competition."

"Competition!" Her eyes flared wide open and she looked at me like she never seen me before. "Do you mean, that you-that I-that-"

"Well," I said modestly, "everybody on Bear Creek is just wonderin' when you're goin' to set the day for us to git hitched. You see gals don't stay single very long in these parts, and-hey, what's the matter?"

Because she was getting paler and paler like she'd et something which didn't agree with her.

"Nothing," she said faintly. "You-you mean people are expecting me to marry you?"

"Shore," I said.

She muttered something that sounded like "My God!" and licked her lips with her tongue and looked at me like she was about ready to faint. Well, it ain't every gal which has a chance to get hitched to Breckinridge Elkins, so I didn't blame her for being excited.

"You've been very kind to me, Breckinridge," she said feebly. "But I-this is so sudden-so unexpected-I never thought-I never dreamed-"

11

"I don't want to rush you," I said. "Take yore time. Next week will be soon enough. Anyway, I got to build us a cabin, and-"

Bang! went a gun, too loud for a Winchester.

"Elkins!" It was J. Pembroke yelling for me up the slope. "Elkins! Hurry!"

"Who's that?" she exclaimed, jumping to her feet like she was working on a spring.

"Aw," I said in disgust, "it's a fool tenderfoot Bill Glanton wished on me. I reckon a b'ar is got him by the neck. I'll go see."

"I'll go with you!" she said, but from the way Pembroke was yelling I figgered I better not waste no time getting to him, so I couldn't wait for her, and she was some piece behind me when I mounted the lap of the slope and met him running out from amongst the trees. He was gibbering with excitement.

"I winged it!" he squawked. "I'm sure I winged the blighter! But it ran in among the underbrush and I dared not follow it, for the beast is most vicious when wounded. A friend of mine once wounded one in South Africa, and-"

"A b'ar?" I ast.

"No, no!" he said. "A wild boar! The most vicious brute I have ever seen! It ran into that brush there!"

"Aw, they ain't no wild boars in the Humbolts," I snorted. "You wait here. I'll go see just what you did shoot."

I seen some splashes of blood on the grass, so I knowed he'd shot something. Well, I hadn't gone more'n a few hunderd feet and was just out of sight of J. Pembroke when I run into Uncle Jeppard Grimes.

Uncle Jeppard was one of the first white men to come into the Humbolts. He's as lean and hard as a pine-knot, and wears fringed buckskins and moccasins just like he done fifty years ago. He had a bowie knife in one hand and he waved something in the other'n like a flag of revolt, and he was frothing at the mouth.

"The derned murderer!" he howled. "You see this? That's the tail of Daniel Webster, the finest derned razorback boar which ever trod the Humbolts! That danged tenderfoot of your'n tried to kill him! Shot his tail off, right spang up to the hilt! He cain't muterlate my animals like this! I'll have his heart's blood!"

And he done a war-dance waving that pig-tail and his bowie and cussing in English and Spanish and Apache Injun an at once.

"You ca'm down, Uncle Jeppard," I said sternly. "He ain't got no sense, and he thought Daniel Webster was a wild boar like they have in Aferker and England and them foreign places. He didn't mean no harm."

"No harm!" said Uncle Jeppard fiercely. "And Daniel Webster with no more tail onto him than a jackrabbit!"

"Well," I said, "here's a five dollar gold piece to pay for the dern hawg's tail, and you let J. Pembroke alone."

"Gold cain't satisfy honor," he said bitterly, but nevertheless grabbing the coin like a starving man grabbing a beefsteak. "I'll let this outrage pass for the time. But I'll be watchin' that maneyack to see that he don't muterlate no more of my prize razorbacks."

And so saying he went off muttering in his beard.

I WENT BACK TO WHERE I left J. Pembroke, and there he was talking to Miss Margaret which had just come up. She had more color in her face than I'd saw recent.

"Fancy meeting a girl like you here!" J. Pembroke was saying.

"No more surprizing than meeting a man like you!" says she with a kind of fluttery laugh.

"Oh, a sportsman wanders into all sorts of out-of-the-way places," says he, and seeing they hadn't noticed me coming up, I says: "Well, J. Pembroke, I didn't find yore wild boar, but I met the owner."

He looked at me kinda blank, and said vaguely: "Wild boar? What wild boar?"

"That-un you shot the tail off of with that there fool elerfant gun," I said. "Listen: next time you see a hawg-critter you remember there ain't no wild boars in the Humbolts. They is critters called haverleeners in South Texas, but they ain't even none of them in Nevada. So next time you see

14

a hawg, just reflect that it's merely one of Uncle Jeppard Grimes' razorbacks and refrain from shootin' at it."

"Oh, quite!" he agreed absently, and started talking to Miss Margaret again.

So I picked up the elerfant gun which he'd absent-mindedly laid down, and said: "Well, it's gittin' late. Let's go. We won't go back to pap's cabin tonight, J. Pembroke. We'll stay at Uncle Saul Garfield's cabin on t'other side of the Apache Mountain settlement."

As I said, them cabins was awful close together. Uncle Saul's cabin was below the settlement, but it warn't much over three hundred yards from cousin Bill Kirby's cabin where Miss Margaret boarded. The other cabins was on t'other side of Bill's, mostly, strung out up the run, and up and down the slopes.

I told J. Pembroke and Miss Margaret to walk on down to the settlement whilst I went back and got the horses.

They'd got to the settlement time I catched up with 'em, and Miss Margaret had gone into the Kirby cabin, and I seen a light spring up in her room. She had one of them new-fangled ile lamps she brung with her, the only one on Bear Creek. Candles and pine chunks was good enough for us folks. And she'd hanged rag things over the winders which she called curtains. You never seen nothing like it, I tell you she was that elegant you wouldn't believe it.

We walked on toward Uncle Saul's, me leading the horses, and after a while J. Pembroke says: "A wonderful creature!"

"You mean Daniel Webster?" I ast.

"No!" he said. "No, no, I mean Miss Ashley."

"She shore is," I said. "She'll make me a fine wife."

He whirled like I'd stabbed him and his face looked pale in the dusk.

"You?" he said, "You a wife?"

"Well," I said bashfully, "she ain't sot the day yet, but I've shore sot my heart on that gal."

"Oh!" he says, "Oh!" says he, like he had the toothache. Then he said kinda hesitatingly: "Suppose-er, just suppose, you know! Suppose a rival for her affections should appear? What would you do?"

"You mean if some dirty, low-down son of a mangy skunk was to try to steal my gal?" I said, whirling so sudden he staggered backwards.

"Steal my gal?" I roared, seeing red at the mere thought. "Why, I'd-I'd-"

Words failing me I wheeled and grabbed a good-sized sapling and tore it up by the roots and broke it across my knee and throwed the pieces clean through a rail fence on the other side of the road.

"That there is a faint idee!" I said, panting with passion.

"That gives me a very good conception," he said faintly, and he said nothing more till we reached the cabin and seen Uncle Saul Garfield standing in the light of the door combing his black beard with his fingers.

NEXT MORNING J. PEMBROKE seemed like he'd kinda lost interest in b'ars. He said all that walking he done over the slopes of Apache Mountain had made his laig muscles sore. I never heard of such a thing, but nothing that gets the matter with these tenderfeet surprizes me much, they is such a effemernate race, so I ast him would he like to go fishing down the run and he said all right.

But we hadn't been fishing more'n a hour when he said he believed he'd go back to Uncle Saul's cabin and take him a nap, and he insisted on going alone, so I stayed where I was and ketched me a nice string of trout.

I went back to the cabin about noon, and ast Uncle Saul if J. Pembroke had got his nap out.

"Why, heck," said Uncle Saul. "I ain't seen him since you and him started down the run this mornin'. Wait a minute-yonder he comes from the other direction."

Well, J. Pembroke didn't say where he'd been all morning, and I didn't ast him, because a tenderfoot don't generally have no reason for anything he does.

We et the trout I ketched, and after dinner he perked up a right smart and got his shotgun and said he'd like to hunt some wild turkeys. I never heard of anybody hunting anything as big as a turkey with a shotgun, but I didn't say nothing, because tenderfeet is like that.

So we headed up the slopes of Apache Mountain, and I stopped by the schoolhouse to tell Miss Margaret I probably wouldn't get back in time to take my reading and writing lesson, and she said: "You know, until I met your friend, Mr. Pembroke, I didn't realize what a difference there was between men like him, and-well, like the men on Bear Creek."

"I know," I said. "But don't hold it agen him. He means well. He just ain't got no sense. Everybody cain't be smart like me. As a special favor to me, Miss Margaret, I'd like for you to be exter nice to the poor sap, because he's a friend of my friend Bill Glanton down to War Paint."

"I will, Breckinridge," she replied heartily, and I thanked her and went away with my big manly heart pounding in my gigantic bosom.

Me and J. Pembroke headed into the heavy timber, and we hadn't went far till I was convinced that somebody was follering us. I kept hearing twigs snapping, and oncet I thought I seen a shadowy figger duck behind a bush. But when I run back there, it was gone, and no track to show in the pine needles. That sort of thing would of made me nervous, anywhere else, because they is a awful lot of people which would like to get a clean shot at my back from the bresh, but I knowed none of them dast come after me in my own territory. If anybody was trailing us it was bound to be one of my relatives and to save my neck I couldn't think of no reason why anyone of 'em would be gunning for me.

But I got tired of it, and left J. Pembroke in a small glade while I snuck back to do some shaddering of my own. I aimed to cast a big circle around the opening and see could I find out who it was, but I'd hardly got out of sight of J. Pembroke when I heard a gun bang.

I turned to run back and here come J. Pembroke yelling: "I got him! I got him! I winged the bally aborigine!"

He had his head down as he busted through the bresh and he run into me in his excitement and hit me in the belly with his head so hard he bounced back like a rubber ball and landed in a bush with his riding boots brandishing wildly in the air.

"Assist me, Breckinridge!" he shrieked. "Extricate me! They will be hot on our trail!"

"Who?" I demanded, hauling him out by the hind laig and setting him on his feet.

"The Indians!" he hollered, jumping up and down and waving his smoking shotgun frantically. "The bally redskins! I shot one of them! I saw him sneaking through the bushes! I saw his legs! I know it was an Indian because he had on moccasins instead of boots! Listen! That's him now!"

"A Injun couldn't cuss like that," I said. "You've shot Uncle Jeppard Grimes!"

19

TELLING HIM TO STAY there, I run through the bresh, guided by the maddened howls which riz horribly on the air, and busting through some bushes I seen Uncle Jeppard rolling on the ground with both hands clasped to the rear bosom of his buckskin britches which was smoking freely. His langwidge was awful to hear.

"Air you in misery, Uncle Jeppard?" I inquired solicitously. This evoked another ear-splitting squall.

"I'm writhin' in my death-throes," he says in horrible accents, "and you stands there and mocks my mortal agony! My own blood-kin!" he says. "ae-ae-ae-ae!" says Uncle Jeppard with passion.

"Aw," I says, "that there bird-shot wouldn't hurt a flea. It cain't be very deep under yore thick old hide. Lie on yore belly, Uncle Jeppard," I said, stropping my bowie on my boot, "and I'll dig out them shot for you."

"Don't tech me!" he said fiercely, painfully climbing onto his feet. "Where's my rifle-gun? Gimme it! Now then, I demands that you bring that English murderer here where I can git a clean lam at him! The Grimes honor is besmirched and my new britches is rooint. Nothin' but blood can wipe out the stain on the family honor!"

"Well," I said, "you hadn't no business sneakin' around after us thataway-"

Here Uncle Jeppard give tongue to loud and painful shrieks.

"Why shouldn't I?" he howled. "Ain't a man got no right to pertect his own property? I was follerin' him to see that he didn't shoot no more tails offa my hawgs. And now he shoots me in the same place! He's a fiend in human form-a monster which stalks ravelin' through these hills bustin' for the blood of the innercent!"

"Aw, J. Pembroke thought you was a Injun," I said.

"He thought Daniel Webster was a wild wart-hawg," gibbered Uncle Jeppard. "He thought I was Geronimo. I reckon he'll massacre the entire population of Bear Creek under a misapprehension, and you'll uphold and defend him! When the cabins of yore kinfolks is smolderin' ashes, smothered in the blood of yore own relatives, I hope you'll be satisfied-bringin' a foreign assassin into a peaceful community!"

Here Uncle Jeppard's emotions choked him, and he chawed his whiskers and then yanked out the five-dollar gold piece I give him for Daniel Webster's tail, and throwed it at me.

"Take back yore filthy lucre," he said bitterly. "The day of retribution is close onto hand, Breckinridge Elkins, and the Lord of battles shall jedge between them which turns agen their kinfolks in their extremerties!"

"In their which?" I says, but he merely snarled and went limping off through the trees, calling back over his shoulder: "They is still men on Bear Creek which will see justice did for the aged and helpless. I'll git that English murderer if it's the last thing I do, and you'll be sorry you stood up for him, you big lunkhead!"

I went back to where J. Pembroke was waiting bewilderedly, and evidently still expecting a tribe of Injuns to bust out of the bresh and sculp him, and I said in disgust: "Let's go home. Tomorrer I'll take you so far away from Bear Creek you can shoot in any direction without hittin' a prize razorback or a antiquated gunman with a ingrown disposition. When Uncle Jeppard Grimes gits mad enough to throw away money, it's time to ile the Winchesters and strap your scabbard-ends to yore laigs."

"Legs?" he said mistily, "But what about the Indian?"

"There warn't no Injun, gol-dern it!" I howled. "They ain't been any on Bear Creek for four or five year. They-aw, hell! What's the use? Come on. It's gittin' late. Next time you see somethin' you don't understand, ast me before you shoot it. And remember, the more ferocious and woolly it looks, the more likely it is to be a leadin' citizen of Bear Creek."

It was dark when we approached Uncle Saul's cabin, and J. Pembroke glanced back up the road, toward the settlement, and said: "My word, is it a political rally? Look! A torchlight parade!"

I looked, and I said: "Quick! Git into the cabin and stay there."

He turned pale, and said: "If there is danger, I insist on-"

"Insist all you dern please," I said. "But git in that house and stay there. I'll handle this. Uncle Saul, see he gits in there."

Uncle Saul is a man of few words. He taken a firm grip on his pipe stem and grabbed J. Pembroke by the neck and seat of the britches and throwed him bodily into the cabin, and shet the door, and sot down on the stoop.

"They ain't no use in you gittin' mixed up in this, Uncle Saul," I said.

"You got yore faults, Breckinridge," he grunted. "You ain't got much sense, but yo're my favorite sister's son-and I ain't forgot that lame mule Jeppard traded me for a sound animal back in '69. Let 'em come!"

* * *

THEY COME ALL RIGHT, and surged up in front of the cabin-Jeppard's boys Jack and Buck and Esau and Joash and Polk County. And Erath Elkins, and a mob of Gordons and Buckners and Polks, all more or less kin to me, except Joe Braxton who wasn't kin to any of us, but didn't like me because he was sweet on Miss Margaret. But Uncle Jeppard warn't with 'em. Some had torches and Polk County Grimes had a rope with a noose in it.

"Where-at air you all goin' with that there lariat?" I ast them sternly, planting my enormous bulk in their path.

"Perjuice the scoundrel!" said Polk County, waving his rope around his head. "Bring out the foreign invader which shoots hawgs and defenseless old men from the bresh!"

"What you aim to do?" I inquired.

"We aim to hang him!" they replied with hearty enthusiasm.

Uncle Saul knocked the ashes out of his pipe and stood up and stretched his arms which looked like knotted oak limbs, and he grinned in his black beard like a old timber wolf, and he says: "Whar is dear cousin Jeppard to speak for hisself?"

"Uncle Jeppard was havin' the shot picked outa his hide when we left," says Joel Gordon. "He'll be along directly. Breckinridge, we don't want no trouble with you, but we aims to have that Englishman."

"Well," I snorted, "you all cain't. Bill Glanton is trustin' me to return him whole of body and limb, and-"

"What you want to waste time in argyment for, Breckinridge?" Uncle Saul reproved mildly. "Don't you know it's a plumb waste of time to try to reason with the off-spring of a lame-mule trader?"

"What would you suggest, old man?" sneeringly remarked Polk County.

Uncle Saul beamed on him benevolently, and said gently: "I'd try moral suasion-like this!" And he hit Polk County under the jaw and knocked him clean acrost the yard into a rain barrel amongst the ruins of which he reposed until he was rescued and revived some hours later.

But they was no stopping Uncle Saul oncet he took the war-path. No sooner had he disposed of Polk County than he jumped seven foot into the air, cracked his heels together three times, give the rebel yell and come down with his arms around the necks of Esau Grimes and Joe Braxton, which he went to the earth with and starting mopping up the cabin yard with 'em.

That started the fight, and they is no scrap in the world where mayhem is committed as free and fervent as in one of these here family rukuses.

Polk County had hardly crashed into the rain barrel when Jack Grimes stuck a pistol in my face. I slapped it aside just as he fired and the bullet missed me and taken a ear offa Jim Gordon. I was scared Jack would hurt somebody if he kept on shooting reckless that way, so I kinda rapped him with my left fist and how was I to know it would dislocate his jaw. But Jim Gordon seemed to think I was to blame about his ear because he give a maddened howl and jerked up his shotgun and let bam with both barrels. I ducked just in time to keep from getting my head blowed off, and catched most of the double-charge in my shoulder, whilst the rest hived in the seat of Steve Kirby's britches. Being shot that way by a relative was irritating, but I controlled my temper and merely taken the gun away from Jim and splintered the stock over his head.

In the meantime Joel Gordon and Buck Grimes had grabbed one of my laigs apiece and was trying to rassle me to the earth, and Joash Grimes was trying to hold down my right arm, and cousin Pecos Buckner was beating me over the head from behind with a ax-handle, and Erath Elkins was coming at me from the front with a bowie knife. I reached down and got Buck Grimes by the neck with my left hand, and I swung my right and hit Erath with it, but I had to lift Joash clean off his feet and swing him around with the lick, because he wouldn't let go, so I only knocked Erath through the rail fence which was around Uncle Saul's garden.

About this time I found my left laig was free and discovered that Buck Grimes was unconscious, so I let go of his neck and begun to kick around with my left laig and it ain't my fault if the spur got tangled up in Uncle Jonathan Polk's whiskers and jerked most of 'em out by the roots. I shaken Joash off and taken the ax-handle away from Pecos because I seen he was going to hurt somebody if he kept on swinging it around so reckless, and I dunno why he blames me because his skull got fractured when he hit that tree. He oughta look where he falls when he gets throwed across a cabin yard. And if Joel Gordon hadn't been so stubborn trying to gouge me he wouldn't of got his laig broke neither.

I was handicapped by not wanting to kill any of my kinfolks, but they was so mad they all wanted to kill me, so in spite of my carefulness the casualties was increasing at a rate which would of discouraged anybody but Bear Creek folks. But they are the stubbornnest people in the world. Three or four had got me around the laigs again, refusing to be convinced that I couldn't be throwed that way, and Erath Elkins, having pulled hisself out of the ruins of the fence, come charging back with his bowie.

By this time I seen I'd have to use violence in spite of myself, so I grabbed Erath and squoze him with a grizzly-hug and that was when he got them five ribs caved in, and he ain't spoke to me since. I never seen such a cuss for taking offense over trifles.

For a matter of fact, if he hadn't been so bodaciously riled up-if he had of kept his head like I did-he would have seen how kindly I felt toward him even in the fever of that there battle. If I had dropped him underfoot he might have been tromped on fatally for I was kicking folks right and left without caring where they fell. So I carefully flung Erath out of the range of that ruckus-and if he thinks I aimed him at Ozark Grimes and his pitchfork-well, I just never done it. It was Ozark's fault more than mine for toting that pitchfork, and it ought to be Ozark that Erath cusses when he starts to sit down these days.

It was at this moment that somebody swung at me with a ax and ripped my ear nigh offa my head, and I begun to lose my temper. Four or five other relatives was kicking and hitting and biting at me all at oncet, and they is a limit even to my timid manners and mild nature. I voiced my displeasure with a beller of wrath, and lashed out with both fists, and my misguided relatives fell all over the yard like persimmons after a frost. I grabbed Joash Grimes by the ankles and begun to knock them ill-advised idjits in the head with him, and the way he hollered you'd of thought somebody was manhandling him. The yard was beginning to look like a battle-field when the cabin door opened and a deluge of b'iling water descended on us.

I got about a gallon down my neck, but paid very little attention to it, however the others ceased hostilities and started rolling on the ground and hollering and cussing, and Uncle Saul riz up from amongst the ruins of Esau Grimes and Joe Braxton, and bellered: "Woman! What air you at?"

Aunt Zavalla Garfield was standing in the doorway with a kettle in her hand, and she said: "Will you idjits stop fightin'? The Englishman's gone. He run out the back door when the fightin' started, saddled his nag and pulled out. Now will you born fools stop, or will I give you another deluge? Land save us! What's that light?"

Somebody was yelling toward the settlement, and I was aware of a peculiar glow which didn't come from such torches as was still burning. And here come Medina Kirby, one of Bill's gals, yelping like a Comanche.

"Our cabin's burnin'!" she squalled. "A stray bullet went through the winder and busted Miss Margaret's ile lamp!"

WITH A YELL OF DISMAY I abandoned the fray and headed for Bill's cabin, follered by everybody which was able to foller me. They had been several wild shots fired during the melee and one of 'em must have hived in Miss Margaret's winder. The Kirbys had dragged most of their belongings into the yard and some was bringing water from the creek, but the whole cabin was in a blaze by now.

"Whar's Miss Margaret?" I roared.

"She must be still in there!" shrilled Miss Kirby. "A beam fell and wedged her door so we couldn't open it, and-"

I grabbed a blanket one of the gals had rescued and plunged it into the rain barrel and run for Miss Margaret's room. They wasn't but one door in it, which led into the main part of the cabin, and was jammed like they said, and I knowed I couldn't never get my shoulders through either winder, so I just put down my head and rammed the wall full force and knocked four or five logs outa place and made a hole big enough to go through.

The room was so full of smoke I was nigh blinded but I made out a figger fumbling at the winder on the other side. A flaming beam fell outa the roof and broke acrost my head with a loud report and about a bucketful of coals rolled down the back of my neck, but I paid no heed.

I charged through the smoke, nearly fracturing my shin on a bedstead or something, and enveloped the figger in the wet blanket and swept it up in my arms. It kicked wildly and fought and though its voice was muffled in the blanket I ketched some words I never would of thought Miss Margaret would use, but I figgered she was hysterical. She seemed to be wearing spurs, too, because I felt 'em every time she kicked.

By this time the room was a perfect blaze and the roof was falling in and we'd both been roasted if I'd tried to get back to the hole I knocked in the oppersite wall. So I lowered my head and butted my way through the near wall, getting all my eyebrows and hair burnt off in the process, and come staggering through the ruins with my precious burden and fell into the arms of my relatives which was thronged outside.

"I've saved her!" I panted. "Pull off the blanket! Yo're safe, Miss Margaret!"

"ae-ae-ae-ae-ae!" said Miss Margaret, and Uncle Saul groped under the blanket and said: "By golly, if this is the schoolteacher she's growed a remarkable set of whiskers since I seen her last!"

He yanked off the blanket-to reveal the bewhiskered countenance of Uncle Jeppard Grimes!

"Hell's fire!" I bellered. "What you doin' here?"

"I was comin' to jine the lynchin', you blame fool!" he snarled. "I seen Bill's cabin was afire so I clumb in through the back winder to save Miss Margaret. She was gone, but they was a note she'd left. I was fixin' to climb out the winder when this maneyack grabbed me."

"Gimme that note!" I bellered, grabbing it. "Medina! Come here and read it for me."

That note run:

Dear Breckinridge:

I am sorry, but I can't stay on Bear Creek any longer. It was tough enough anyway, but being expected to marry you was the last straw. You've been very kind to me, but it would be too much like marrying a grizzly bear. Please forgive me. I am eloping with J. Pembroke Pemberton. We're going out the back window to avoid any trouble, and ride away on his horse. Give my love to the children. We are going to Europe on our honeymoon.

With love.

Margaret Ashley.

"Now what you got to say?" sneered Uncle Jeppard.

"I'm a victim of foreign entanglements," I said dazedly. "I'm goin' to chaw Bill Glanton's ears off for saddlin' that critter on me. And then I'm goin' to lick me a Englishman if I have to go all the way to Californy to find one."

31

Which same is now my aim, object and ambition. This Englishman took my girl and ruined my education, and filled my neck and spine with burns and bruises. A Elkins never forgets?and the next one that pokes his nose into the Bear Creek country had better be a fighting fool or a powerful fast runner.

www.ingramcontent.com/pod-product-compliance
Lightning Source LLC
Chambersburg PA
CBHW030242180626
46810CB00008B/3258